The Very Hairy Bear

Written by
Beth Shoshan

Illustrated by
Masumi Furukawa

meadowside
CHILDREN'S BOOKS

Here's a bear,
a very hairy bear.

And here's a friend,
the Very Hairy Bear's best friend.

My House

Today, the Very
Hairy Bear
is wondering...

'What will I be
when I grow up?'

'Maybe,' he thinks,
'I could be...

a warm and fluffy Panda Bear?'

'Or a cool and shimmering
Polar Bear!'

'Or maybe,' thinks the
Very Hairy Bear, 'I could be...

a gruff and grumpy Grizzly Bear?'

'Or a sweet
and sticky
Honey Bear!'

'Oh dear!' the Very Sticky
Bear's best friend declares.
'I've never seen a Flower
Bear before!'

And now the Very Hairy Bear,
dressed like a Flowery Honey Bear,
has suddenly got lots and lots
of friends!

'Maybe,' the Very Hairy
Bear yawns, 'for now,
I'll just be a bear...

a very hairy
bear.'

Here's a bear,
a very hairy bear, in a
warm and soapy bath.

And here's a very
hairy little bear...

tucked up snug
in bed.

For Steph
- my best friend, my basherte,
my soulmate!

B.S.

For Yasushi & Micia

M.F.

First published in 2011
by Meadowside Children's Books,
185 Fleet Street, London EC4A 2HS
www.meadowsidebooks.com

Text © Beth Shoshan 2011
Illustrations © Masumi Furukawa 2011

The rights of Beth Shoshan and Masumi Furukawa
to be identified as the author and illustrator of this work
have been asserted by them in accordance with
the Copyright, Designs and Patents Act, 1988

A CIP catalogue record for this book is available from the British Library
1 2 3 4 5 6 7 8 9 10

Paper used in the production of this book is a natural,
recyclable product from wood grown in sustainable forests

Printed in China